English translation copyright © 2001, 2007 Abbeville Press.
Copyright © 1998 Editions Nathan (Paris–France) for the first edition. Copyright © 2006
Editions Nathan (Paris–France) for the current edition. Original edition: *Lutins Et Cordonnier.*
Translated by Molly Stevens. All rights reserved under international copyright conventions.
No part of this book may be reproduced or utilized in any form or by any means,
electronic or mechanical, including photocopying, recording, or by any storage and
retrieval system, without permission in writing from the publisher. Inquiries should be
addressed to Abbeville Publishing Group, 137 Varick Street, New York, NY 10013.
The text of this book was set in Berkeley Book. Printed and bound in China.

First edition
2 4 6 8 10 9 7 5 3
ISBN-13: 978-0-7892-0731-9
ISBN-10: 0-7892-0731-1

Library of Congress Cataloging-in-Publication Data
Grimm, Jacob, 1785-1863.
The elves and the shoemaker : a fairy tale / by the brothers Grimm ;
illustrated by Dominique Thibault ; [translated by Molly Stevens]. — 1st ed.
p. cm. — (Little pebbles)
Summary: A pair of industrious elves bring prosperity to a
kindly shoemaker and his wife.
ISBN 0-7892-0731-1 (alk. paper)
[1. Fairy Tales. 2. Folklore — Germany.] I. Grimm, Wilhelm, 1786-1859.
II. Thibault, Dominique, ill. III. Stevens, Molly. IV. Wichtelmanner. English.
V. Title. VI. Series
PZ8.G882 Ek 2001
398.2'0943'02—dc21
[E]   2001022970

For bulk and premium sales and for text adoption procedures,
write to Customer Service Manager,
Abbeville Press, 137 Varick Street, New York, NY 10013, or call 1-800-ARTBOOK.

Visit Abbeville Press online at www.abbeville.com.

The Elves and the Shoemaker

A Fairy Tale by the Brothers Grimm
Illustrated by Dominique Thibault

· Abbeville Kids ·

A Division of Abbeville Publishing Group

New York · London

Once upon a time there was a shoemaker. Although he worked hard, he had very bad luck and became poorer and poorer. Finally all he had left was a piece of leather large enough to make just one pair of shoes. He cut out the pieces and prepared to sew them together. Then, because it was late, he left the pieces on his worktable and went upstairs to bed.

Early the next morning he entered his shop.
When he looked at the worktable, the leather
pieces were gone. In their place stood a beautiful
pair of shoes!

The shoemaker rubbed his eyes in disbelief, then
he called his wife in. She was just as surprised
as he was. They looked for clues that would help
them figure out who had made the shoes, but
they didn't find any. So they put the shoes in the
shop window.

Just then a finely dressed gentleman came in. He admired the handsome shoes and bought them on the spot. Because they were so well made, he was happy to offer extra money for them.

The shoemaker took the money and bought enough leather and supplies to make two pairs of shoes. He cut out the pieces and placed them on the worktable. Then he went to bed.

When the shoemaker and his wife entered the shop the next morning, there, on the worktable, were two pairs of shoes.

"How amazing!" exclaimed the shoemaker's wife.

"Remarkable!" replied the shoemaker. "And just look at how well they are made.

The stitching is just as fine as it was on the shoes we found yesterday."

The shoemaker and his wife were still admiring the new shoes when a lady and a gentleman walked in. They thought the shoes were wonderful, and they bought them before any other customers came in. With the money, the shoemaker was able to buy enough leather for four pairs of shoes.

It was late in the day again when the honest shoemaker cut the leather into pieces.

Just as he had done before, he left the pieces on his worktable and went to bed. When he awoke the next day, he found four pairs of shoes!

This strange but wonderful pattern continued for several weeks. Every evening the shoemaker would cut out the leather pieces, and in the morning he would find finished pairs of shoes.

There were all kinds of shoes, too—shoes with laces, shoes with straps; shoes with high heels and shoes that were flat; delicate slippers and sturdy boots.

The mysterious shoemaker could make anything! Around the town word spread about the beautiful shoes and customers flocked to the shoemaker's shop. He and his wife were no longer poor. In fact, they became very prosperous.

One night, two days before Christmas, the shoemaker said to his wife, "Let's stay up tonight and see who has been so kind to us." His wife quickly agreed.

So the shoemaker put the leather pieces on the worktable and then he and his wife hid behind a curtain.

As the clock struck midnight, they saw two tiny elves squeeze through the slats in the shutters. Even though it was cold outside, they had no clothes on! The elves sat down at the worktable and set to work. Zzz, zzz went the thread. Tap, tap went the hammers. How quickly they worked! In almost no time at all they had finished a pair of shoes.

The elves kept working until they had made shoes from all the leather on the worktable. Then they ran out through the shutters into the cold night.

The shoemaker and his wife looked at each other in amazement.

"How can we thank these elves for all they have done for us?" asked the shoemaker.

"They have nothing to wear, and it is winter," said his wife. "I will make them some fine clothes."

"And I will make each of them a pair of shoes," said the shoemaker.

They worked all day. The wife sewed two tiny green jackets, two tiny yellow vests, two tiny pairs of white pants, and two little red caps with feathers. Her husband made two tiny pairs of handsome, pointy-toed shoes. He decorated them with shiny buttons. Finally, everything was ready, and just in time—it was Christmas Eve.

The shoemaker cleaned off his worktable and placed the handsome clothes where he usually laid out the pieces of leather. Then he and his wife hid behind the curtain to see what would happen.

At midnight the elves came skipping over to the table. They were ready to start work when they spotted the clothes and stopped in their tracks.

How surprised they were! Quickly they put on their new clothes. Everything fit perfectly!

Then the elves began leaping and dancing and singing:

Now that we look so fine and neat,

We'll celebrate Christmas and play in the street!

They were still singing this song as they skipped out of the shop, never to return.

The shoemaker and his wife smiled at each other. They were pleased that their gifts had made the elves so happy.

Thanks to the elves, the shoemaker now had many customers. He and his wife were never poor again.

All of these objects appear somewhere in the book.
Can you find them?